WELCOME TO
PASSPORT TO READING
A beginning reader's ticket to a brand-new world!

Every book in this program is designed to build read-along and read-alone skills, level by level, through engaging and enriching stories. As the reader turns each page, he or she will become more confident with new vocabulary, sight words, and comprehension.

These PASSPORT TO READING levels will help you choose the perfect book for every reader.

READING TOGETHER
Read short words in simple sentence structures together to begin a reader's journey.

READING OUT LOUD
Encourage developing readers to sound out words in more complex stories with simple vocabulary.

READING INDEPENDENTLY
Newly independent readers gain confidence reading more complex sentences with higher word counts.

READY TO READ MORE
Readers prepare for chapter books with fewer illustrations and longer paragraphs.

This book features sight words from the educator-supported Dolch Sight Words List. This encourages the reader to recognize commonly used vocabulary words, increasing reading speed and fluency.

For more information, please visit passporttoreadingbooks.com.

Enjoy the journey!

© 2017 MARVEL © 2017 CPIII
Illustrations by Steve Kurth, Andy Smith, and Chris Sotomayor

Cover design by Carolyn Bull.

Little, Brown and Company
Hachette Book Group
1290 Avenue of the Americas, New York, NY 10104
Visit us at lb-kids.com
marvelkids.com

First Edition: June 2017

Little, Brown and Company is a division of Hachette Book Group, Inc. The Little, Brown name and logo are trademarks of Hachette Book Group, Inc.

The publisher is not responsible for websites (or their content) that are not owned by the publisher.

ISBNs: 978-0-316-43834-6 (pbk.), 978-0-316-47619-5 (Scholastic ed.), 978-0-316-43837-7 (ebook), 978-0-316-43836-0 (ebook), 978-0-316-43835-3 (ebook)

Printed in the United States of America

CW

10 9 8 7 6 5 4 3 2

Passport to Reading titles are leveled by independent reviewers applying the standards developed by Irene Fountas and Gay Su Pinnell in *Matching Books to Readers: Using Leveled Books in Guided Reading*, Heinemann, 1999.

MARVEL
SPIDER-MAN
HOMECOMING

Meet
Spidey

Adapted by Charles Cho

Illustrations by Steve Kurth, Andy Smith, and Chris Sotomayor
Directed by Jon Watts
Produced by Kevin Feige and Amy Pascal
Based on the Screenplay by
Jonathan Goldstein & John Francis Daley
and Jon Watts & Christopher Ford
and Chris McKenna & Erik Sommers

LITTLE, BROWN AND COMPANY
New York   Boston

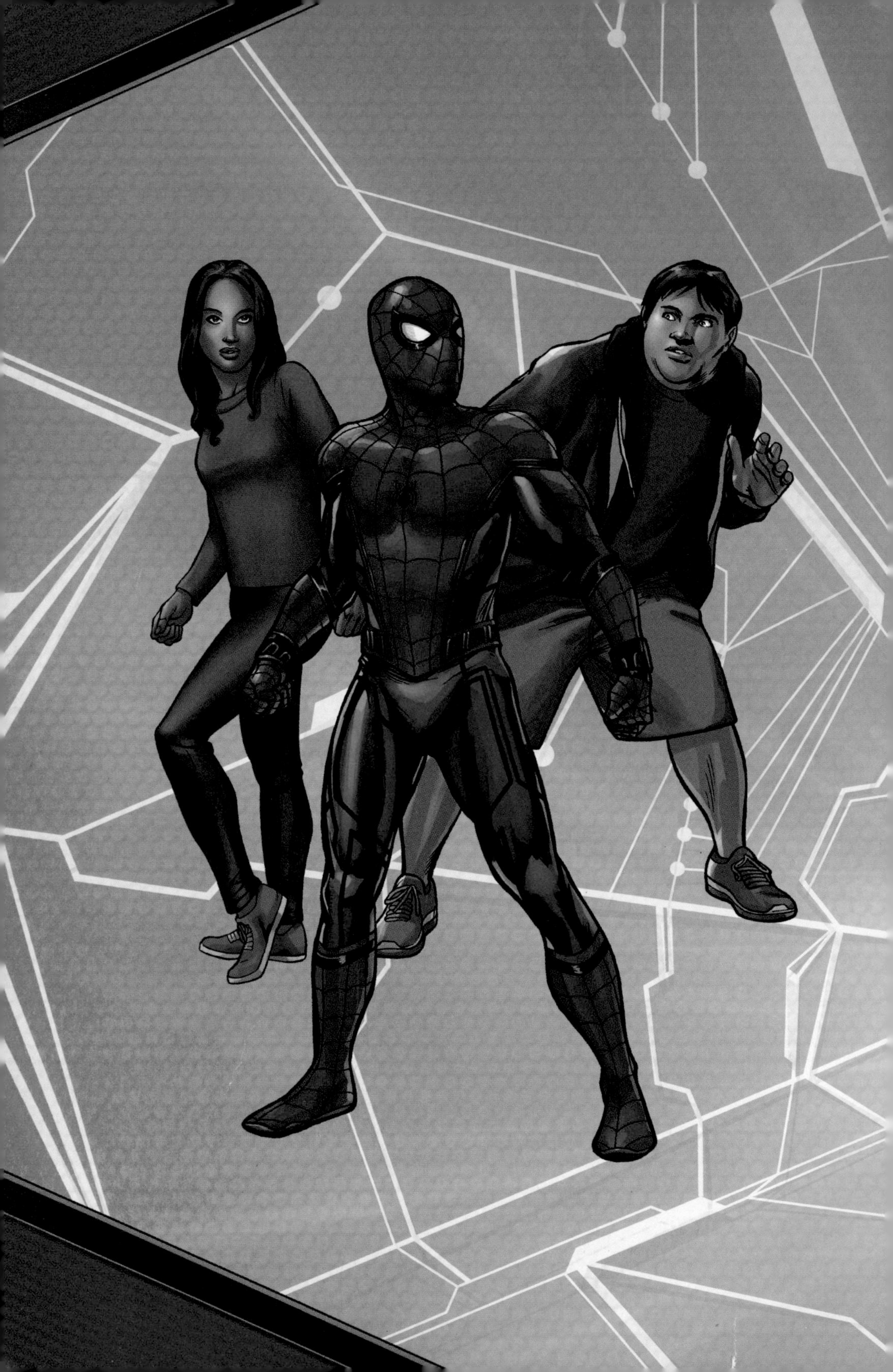

Attention, SPIDER-MAN fans!
Look for these words when you read
this book. Can you spot them all?

sandwiches

bicycle

weapon

restaurant

Spider-Man is really Peter Parker.
He lives with May in Queens.

Peter goes to school like any normal kid.

His favorite subject is science.

He is really good at it!

One of Peter's classmates is Flash.

He thinks he is cool,

but he is really just mean.

He is Peter's rival.

Ned is Peter's friend.

In fact, Ned is Peter's best friend!

They eat lunch together every day

and hang out after school.

They like to build models

of the solar system.

Peter, Ned, Michelle, Liz, and Flash are members of the school's decathlon team.

Their teacher Mr. Harrington
helps them get ready for a big meet,
where they will take quizzes.
Peter cannot go to the meet.
He has to be Spider-Man!

Spidey needs webs to be a hero.

Peter makes them in the chemistry lab.

He has to be careful so no one sees

what he is doing!

Peter tells people he works in another lab when he is really out saving people.

Tony Stark owns the lab.

Tony is a smart and rich engineer.

He is also an Avenger!

Tony Stark is Iron Man!

Spider-Man also needs food for energy.
Peter buys sandwiches and
gummy worms from Mr. Dalmar.
They are yummy!

Peter is ready to be Spider-Man!
He puts on his uniform in an alley.
It looks good.

Someone is stealing a bicycle!
Spidey can stop him.

THWIP! He covers the bad guy in webbing.
Then Spider-Man makes sure
no one will steal the bicycle again!

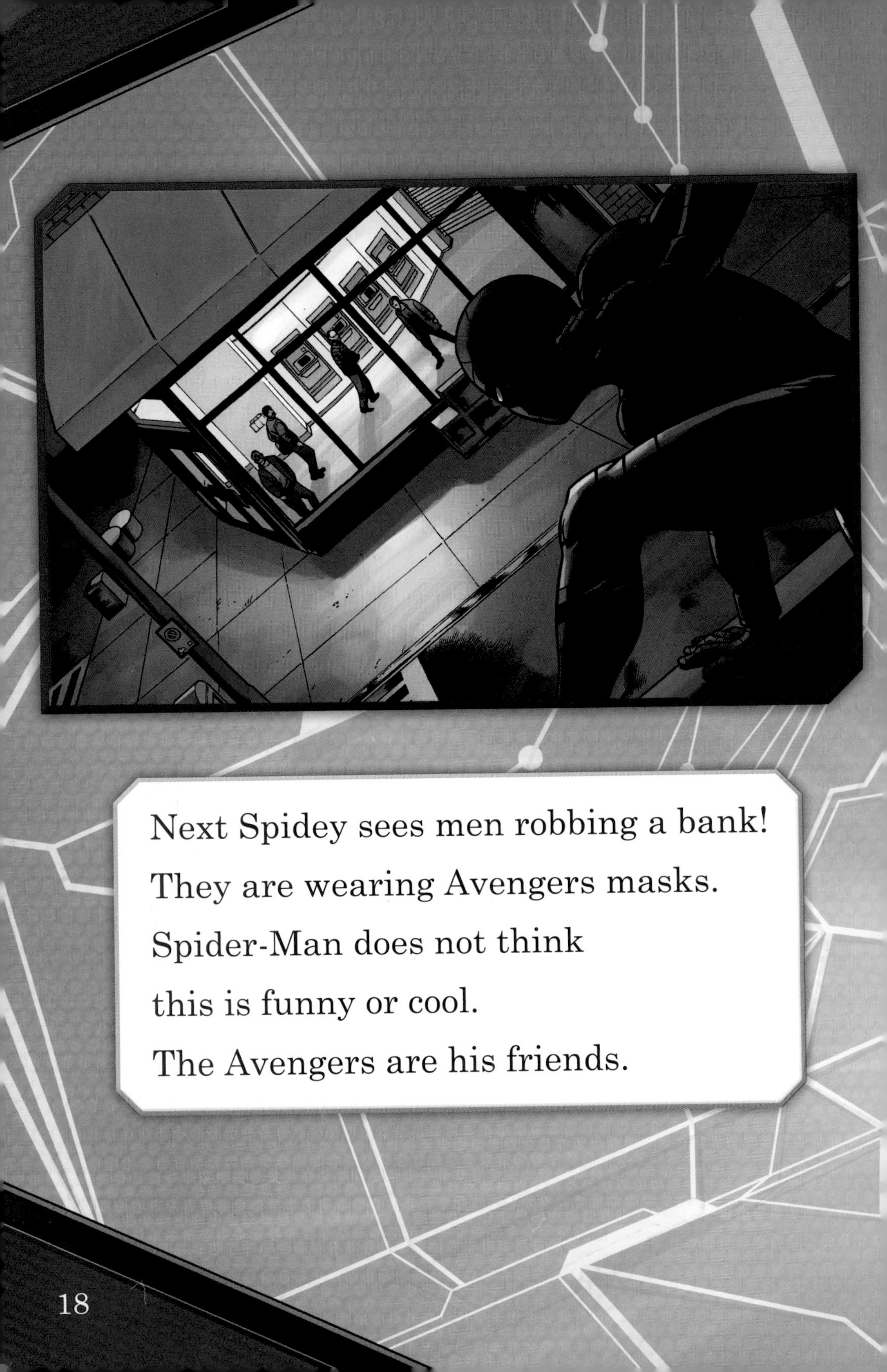

Next Spidey sees men robbing a bank!
They are wearing Avengers masks.
Spider-Man does not think
this is funny or cool.
The Avengers are his friends.

Spider-Man swings in to stop the crime!
The bad guys are surprised.
Spidey shoots webs at the fake Hulk.

Then Spider-Man leaps at the man wearing the Iron Man mask. Money flies everywhere!

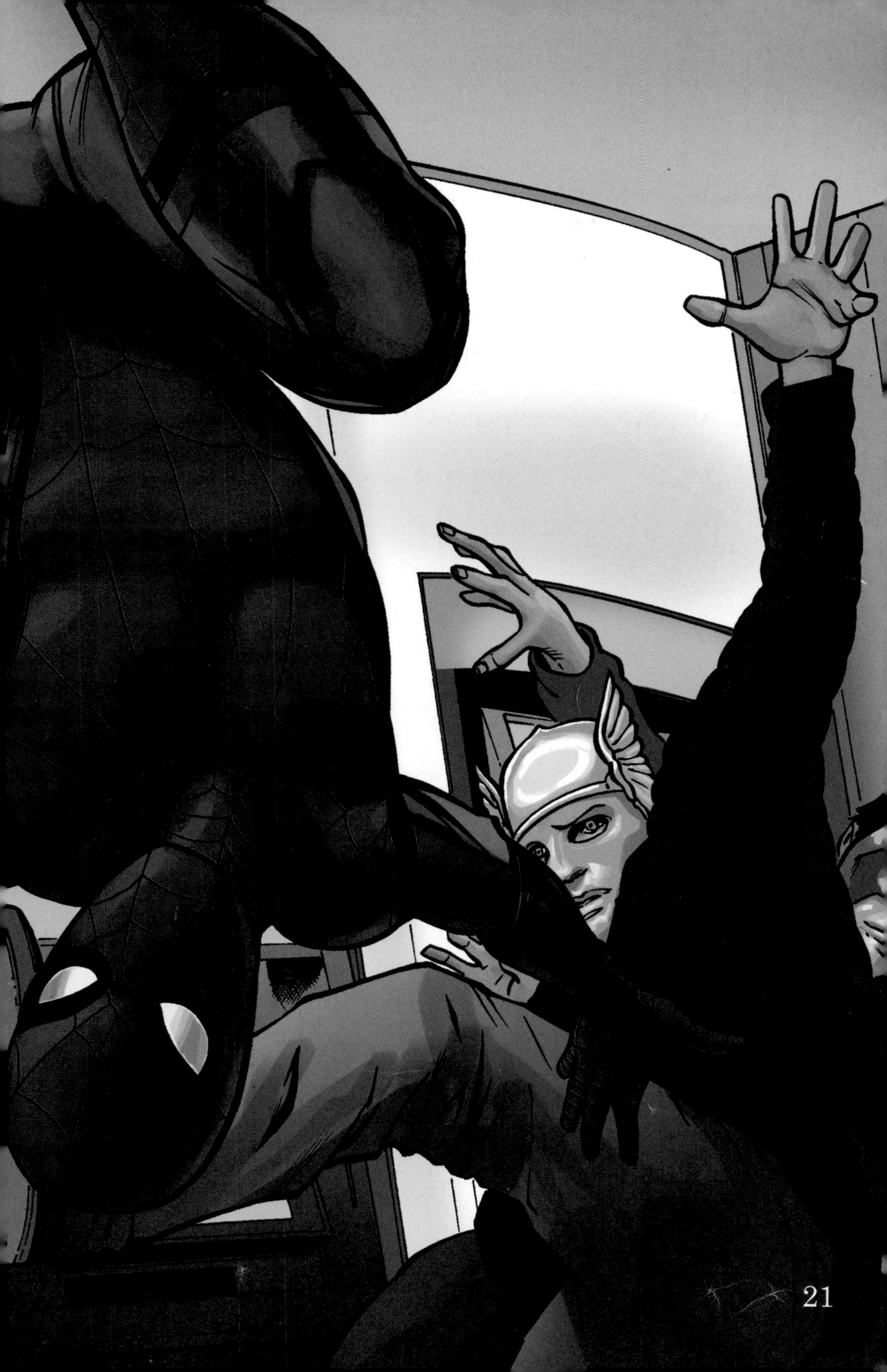

The bad guys fight back.
The man in the Iron Man mask
fires a strange weapon at Spider-Man.
He moves out of the way just in time!

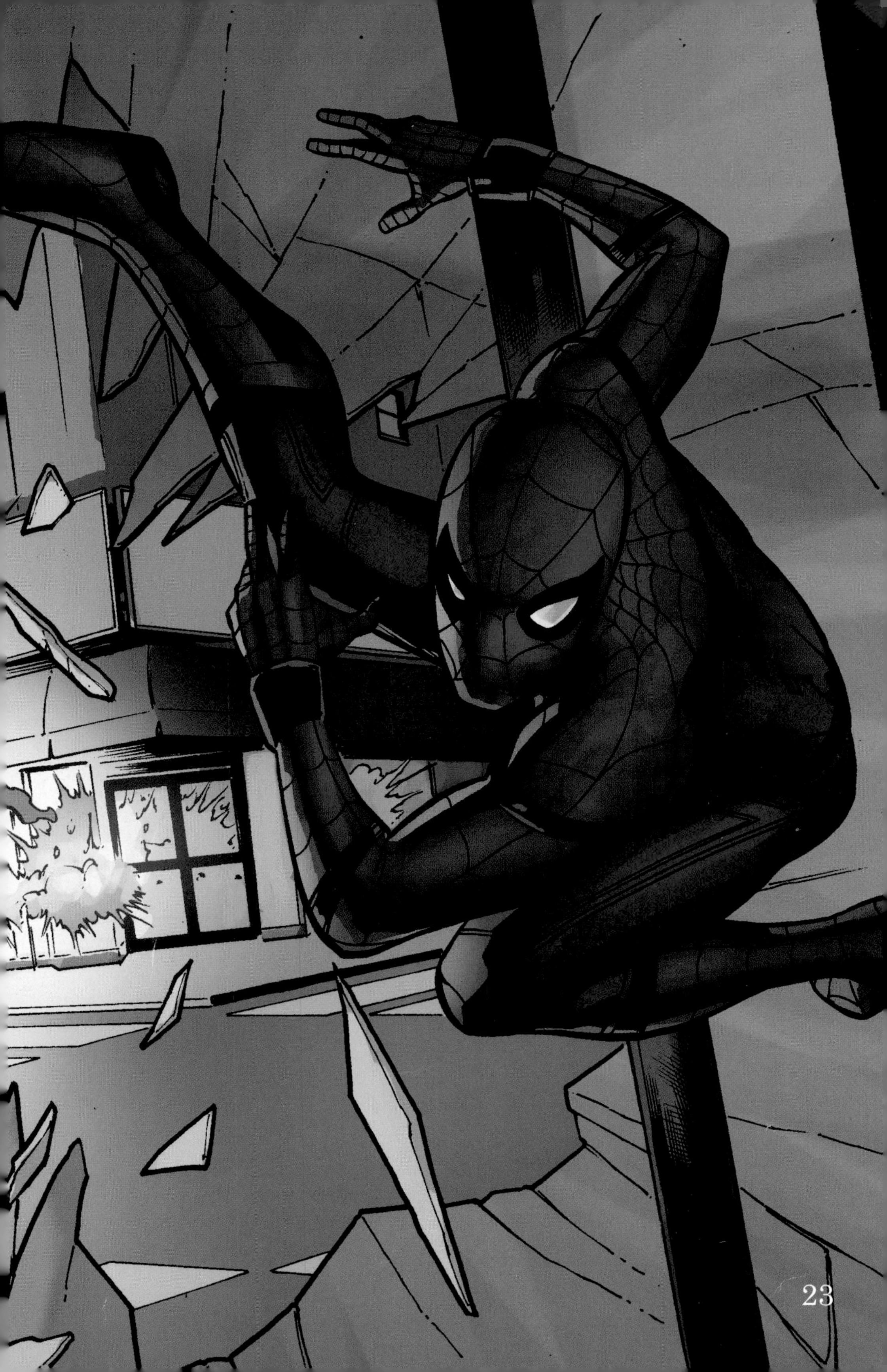

Oh no!
The energy blast hits
Mr. Dalmar's store!

It is ruined, but Mr. Dalmar is okay.
Spider-Man is sad and mad.

It is time for Peter to take off
the Spider-Man uniform and eat dinner.
May takes him to a restaurant.
Peter does not act normal.

He thinks about Mr. Dalmar and his store.

He cannot talk about it with May.

She does not know Peter is Spider-Man!

It is a secret.

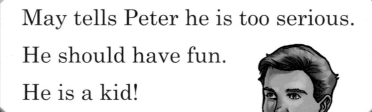

May tells Peter he is too serious.
He should have fun.
He is a kid!

Peter is a good boy and listens to his aunt.

He and Ned will have fun.

They go to a party at Liz's house,

but Spider-Man still has work to do.

So Peter wears his uniform under his clothes!

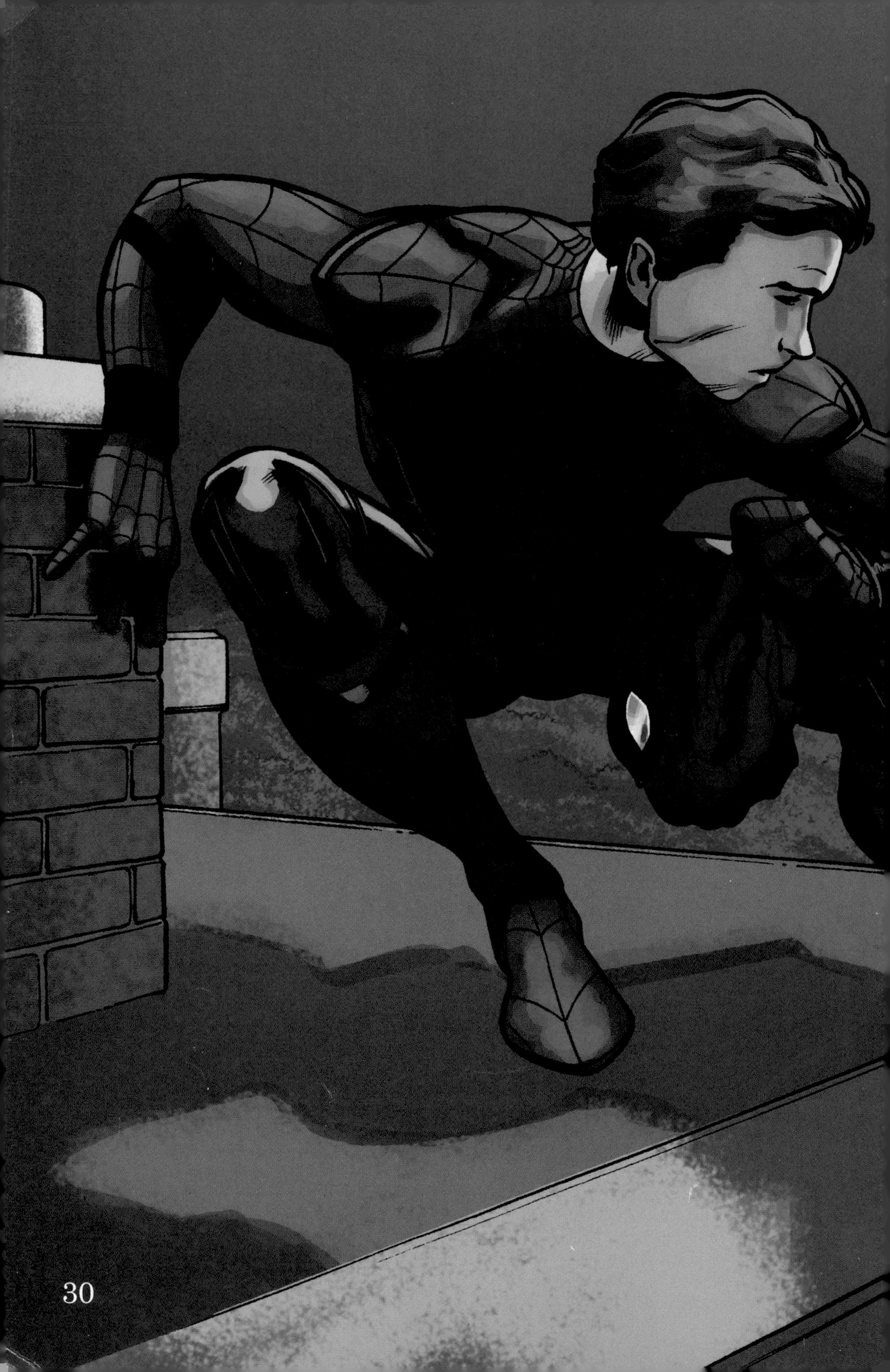

Peter leaves the party
to become Spider-Man.
Peter is on the roof when he sees
an energy burst in the sky.
It is the same kind that destroyed
Mr. Dalmar's store!
What is going on?

Spidey must swing into action
and save the day!
It is a good thing he finished his homework!